Published in the United States by
QEB Publishing, Inc.
23062 La Cadena Drive
Laguna Hills, CA 92653

www.qeb-publishing.com

Library of Congress Control Number has been applied for.

ISBN 978 1 59566 588 1

Author Kate Tym
Illustrator Sarah Wade
Editor Clare Weaver
Designer Alix Wood
Consultant David Hart

Publisher Steve Evans
Creative Director Zeta Davies

Printed and bound in the United States

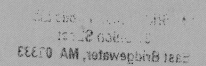

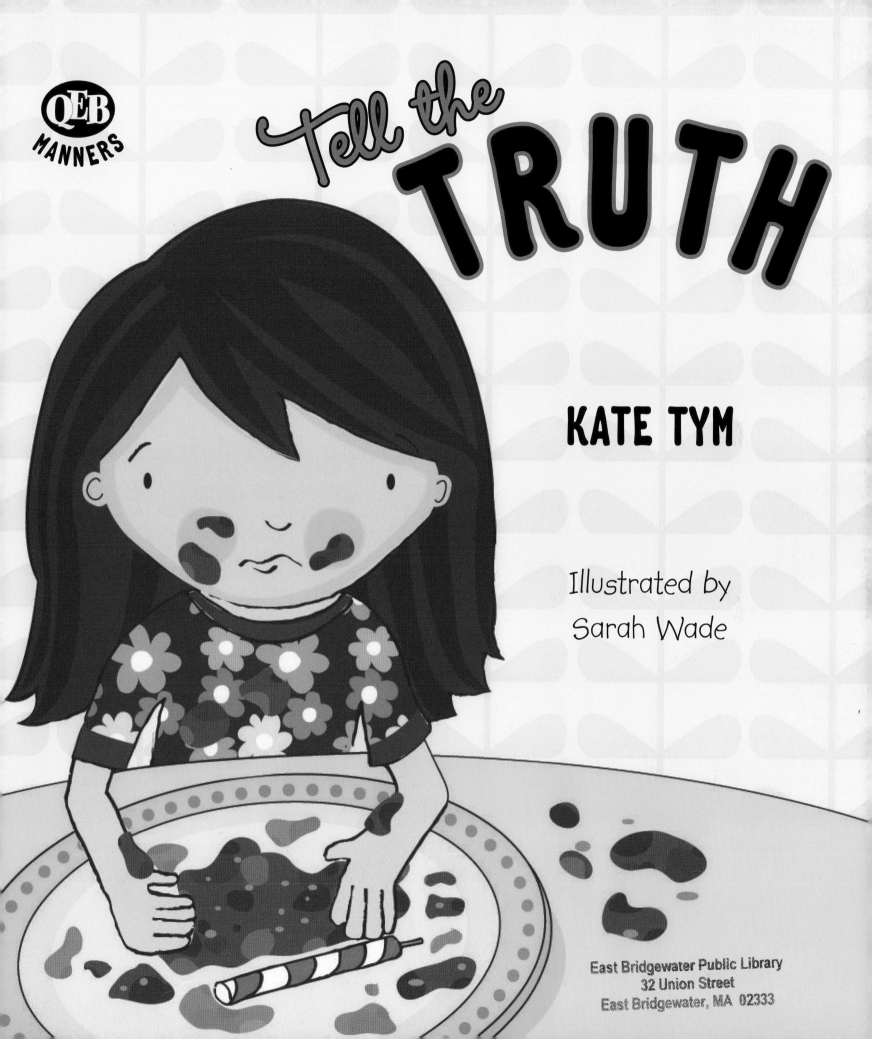

QEB MANNERS

Tell the TRUTH

KATE TYM

Illustrated by

Sarah Wade

Tanya Mortimer's mommy was very good at baking cakes.

When Tanya Mortimer's baby sister was one, her mommy made

the Best Cake EVER

for her birthday party.

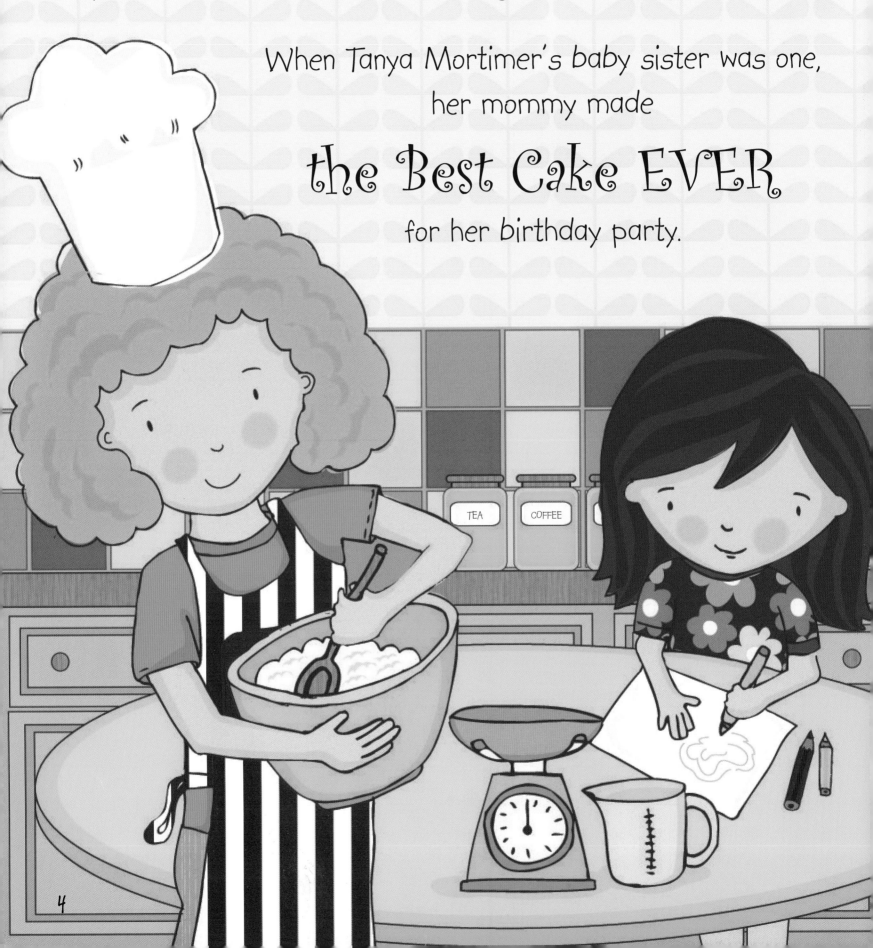

TEA

COFFEE

Mommy left it on the kitchen table and went to wake Baby Brenda from her sleep.

Tanya was left alone in the kitchen with **the Best Cake EVER.**

COFFEE

5

Tanya looked at it. It looked at her.

It seemed to be saying
"Go on Tanya,
have a little bit...
Mommy won't notice
one little bit."

6

Well... thought Tanya.

Yes... thought Tanya.

Perhaps one little bit...
thought Tanya.

Tanya looked at the pile of crumbs that used to be **the Best Cake EVER**.

She felt very bad.

Mommy was going to be really mad.

Mommy was really mad.

ARRRRGH!
Our cake!
Our beautiful CAKE!

"It wasn't me," said Tanya.

"Cake burglars crept in and tried to steal Baby Brenda's cake, and I tried to stop them."

"In fact," said Tanya, "they weren't human burglars. They were **alien** burglars and they **transformogrifacted** themselves into the kitchen.

They had to take the cake, they need sweets to keep their planet **alive**..."

"In fact," said Tanya, "they sucked the cake up into their spaceship using their cake sucker-a-matic machine."

"And I got covered in cake because I jumped on the cake to try and STOP them taking it," said Tanya.

"I was really rather brave."

TEA   COF

13

"You were!" said Mommy. "You were very brave. But this is terrible. We can't have alien burglars coming and stealing our cakes. I must call the police, and the paper, and Daddy!"

Tanya felt terrible. She also felt a bit sick, partly because she'd eaten so much cake and partly because she knew she'd done something really bad.

She'd eaten all the cake and **then** she'd **lied** about it.

NOW Mommy thought she was a **hero** and was going to call the **police!**

15

"Hello," said Mommy, "is that the Chief of Police? Alien burglars came into my kitchen and stole **the Best Cake EVER.** You must investigate at once!"

Tanya felt odd.

Top Cop foils alien burglars!

16

"Hello," said Mommy, "is that the Editor-in-Chief? Alien burglars came into my kitchen and stole **the Best Cake EVER.** My daughter fought them off—you must put it on the **front page!**"

Tanya's knees started to **Wobble**

"Hello," said Mommy, "is that Daddy?

Alien burglars came into the kitchen and stole **the Best Cake EVER.** You must come home **immediately!**"

Tanya couldn't take any more.
"IT WAS ME!" she shouted. "I ate the cake.
There were NO alien burglars,
there was NO transformogrifacation,
there was NO spaceship
and NO cake-sucker-a-matic machine.

And I didn't have to stop them.
I got covered in cake because...
because... because..."

"I ate the cake," said Tanya. "And I'm sorry!"

Mommy looked relieved.

"Thank goodness for that," she said. "I'm glad there aren't any alien cake burglars in our neighborhood and I'm really, really glad you told the truth. That was brave of you."

20

After that, Tanya felt much better.
Then Tanya, Baby Brenda, and Mommy
all baked a brand new cake.

21

When they had finished,
they all had to agree—
this cake really was

the Best Cake EVER
—and that's no lie!

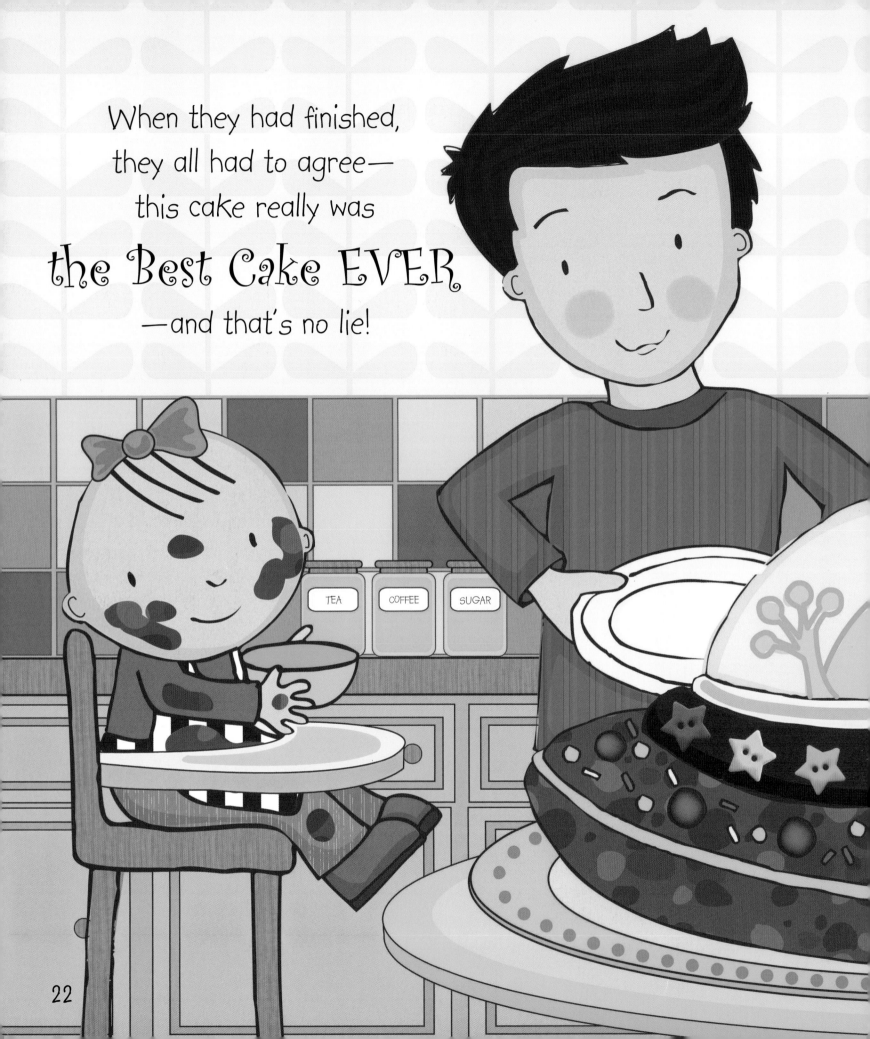

Notes for parents and teachers

- Look at the front cover of the book together. Talk about the picture. Can the children guess what the book is going to be about? Read the title together.

- Read page 6. Discuss with the children what emotion Tanya is feeling when she thinks the cake is talking to her.

- When Tanya looks at the pile of crumbs, why does she feel bad (page 8)? Why does she think Mommy is going to be mad? Talk about trust with the children. Mommy trusted Tanya to be left alone in the kitchen with the cake. Part of trust is doing the right thing when you are left alone.

- Read page 10 together. Why does Tanya say it wasn't her when it was? Point out that although Tanya is worried about getting into trouble for eating the cake, shouldn't she also be worried about getting into trouble for lying? Discuss with the children which is worse, doing something wrong, or lying about it.

- Look at pages 11–13. Talk about the nature of lying with the children—how one lie tends to lead to another and how the hole you dig for yourself can get bigger and bigger.

- On page 15, Tanya has portrayed herself as a hero. Now she feels terrible. Why do the children think she feels like this?

- Discuss pages 16–17 with the children. Mommy calls the police and the newspaper. Tanya's knees start to wobble. Why is this? What will happen if the police and the newspaper people do come to the house? Talk about Tanya having to continue the lie and how things could escalate.

- On page 19, why can't Tanya take it any more? How is trying to keep up the lie making her feel? Do the children think she feels relieved once she's told Mommy? Why isn't Mommy cross? What does Mommy mean when she says it was brave of Tanya to tell the truth?

- Read page 20 together. Discuss the fact that mommies and daddies often know when children are telling lies, which is why it's better not to.

- Tanya's mommy and Baby Brenda all have fun baking a new cake together (page 21). Does Tanya's mommy still love Tanya even though she did something wrong? Explain to the children that parents always love their children no matter what they've done. Sometimes their mommy or daddy may not like what they've done, but they still like them.

- Do the children think Tanya has learned her lesson? Do they think she would lie about something she's done in future?

- Relate the story of the Little Boy who Cried Wolf to the children. What happens if you tell lies all the time?

24